For Simon  For Pascal

A special thank you to Luke,
who did not want to, and then
did. And to Rachel, who adored
Lucy from the beginning.

First published 2009 by Macmillan Children's Books
a division of Macmillan Publishers Limited
20 New Wharf Road, London N1 9RR
Basingstoke and Oxford
Associated companies throughout the world
www.panmacmillan.com
ISBN: 978-0-230-70546-3
Text copyright © Sanchia Oppenheimer 2009
Illustrations copyright © Imogen Clare 2009
Moral rights asserted. All rights reserved.
A CIP catalogue record for this book is available
from the British Library.
Printed in Belgium
9 8 7 6 5 4 3 2 1

Look for me on every page.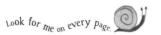

Lucy Goes to Market

Written by Sanchia Oppenheimer

Illustrated by Imogen Clare

MACMILLAN CHILDREN'S BOOKS

Lucy goes to market and finds . . .

an asparagus angel

a Brazilian brass band

a candlelit clock

a delicate dragon

endless

eccentric

eggs

and four flamingos feasting on fruitcake

a groovy garland

half a hedgerow

an
invisible
igloo

just jam

a kimono

and a lopsided lampshade

marmalade moons

a nomad named Nathan

an ordinary orange
and a Persian pillar

quads

with

quilts

a relaxing rainstorm

several strawberries

and a teahouse

a unicorn

umbrella and a vulture with vertigo

wacky wellingtons

yellow
yesterdays

and a zebra.

Lucy is happy with
her doll's house.
Now it is complete.

The End